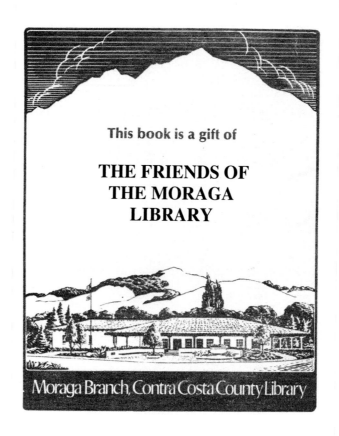

Miss Bindergarten Takes a Field Trip

with Kindergarten

by **JOSEPH SLATE**

illustrated by **ASHLEY WOLFF**

PUFFIN BOOKS

For Milo Ryan,

Lane Smith,

and Greg Spaid—

three gracious steps

J.S.

For Donna Brooks,

Miss Bindergarten's right-paw woman

A.W.

PUFFIN BOOKS
Published by Penguin Group
Penguin Young Readers Group, 345 Hudson Street, New York, New York 10014, U.S.A.
Penguin Books Ltd, 80 Strand, London WC2R ORL, England
Penguin Books Australia Ltd, 250 Camberwell Road, Camberwell, Victoria 3124, Australia
Penguin Books Canada Ltd, 10 Alcorn Avenue, Toronto, Ontario, Canada M4V 3B2
Penguin Books (N.Z.) Ltd, 182-190 Wairau Road, Auckland 10, New Zealand

First published in the United States of America by Dutton Children's Books, a division of Penguin Putnam Books for Young Readers, 2001
Published by Puffin Books, a division of Penguin Young Readers Group, 2004

7 9 10 8 6

CIP Data is available.

Puffin Books ISBN 0-14-240139-0

Printed in the United States of America

Today is field trip day. . . .

Adam's dad's a chaperone.

Brenda's mom is, too.

Christopher says,
"Hey, don't leave yet—
a stone hopped
in my shoe."

Miss Bindergarten goes to the

bakery with kindergarten.

Danny cuts some cookies out.

Emily sees them bake.

Franny squirts pink icing on a scrumptious chocolate cake.

Now Miss Bindergarten goes to the

fire station with kindergarten.

Gwen McGunny
rings a bell.

Henry holds
a hose.

Ian makes a funny face and laughs as his nose grooOWS.

Jessie learns
Stop, Drop, and Roll.

Kiki tries
on gear.

Miss Bindergarten
slides down
the pole, and
Lenny gives a cheer.

Now Miss Bindergarten goes to the

post office with kindergarten.

Matty picks
the planet stamps.

Noah taps
the locks.

Ophelia asks where letters go when you slide them through the slots.

Patricia steers
a canvas cart.

Quentin checks
the scale.

Now Miss Bindergarten goes to the

library with kindergarten.

Sara grabs her favorite chair.

Tommy hugs a book.

Mr. Mack clicks the mouse.
"Here, Ursula, take a look!"

Vicky likes hot-air balloons.

Wanda loves the ships.

"A book is like a ticket to all sorts of splendid trips."

Now Miss Bindergarten goes to the

park with kindergarten.

Xavier shouts,
"Where's Brenda's mom?"

Yolanda looks
behind her.

"Don't worry. She's not lost," says Zach. "I know where we can find her."

Now Miss Bindergarten goes—whoa!

stops!—with kindergarten.

Adam's dad sets out the cups.

Brenda's mom pours punch.

Miss Bindergarten cuts the cake...

. . . and they all sit down

to munch!

Did you see these shapes?

we saw these shapes

at the bakery

we saw these shapes

at the
fire station

circle

square

triangle

rectangle

diamond